I'm afraid of the dark
난 어둠이 무서워

Dominique Curtiss

Muriel Gestin

chouettEDITIONS.com

Tamara
타마라

Moka

모카

"Good night, you two", says Dad, kissing his twins on the forehead.
-잘 자요, 우리 꼬맹이들.
아빠가 쌍둥이의 이마에 입을 맞추며 말합니다.

"Good night, pumpkins", says Mum, kissing her two angels on the cheek. "Sweet dreams."
-잘 자요, 우리 아가들. 좋은 꿈 꾸렴.
엄마가 천사들의 볼에 입을 맞추며 말합니다.

Then she turns off the light as she leaves the room. Click.
딸깍. 엄마가 불을 끄고 방을 나갑니다.

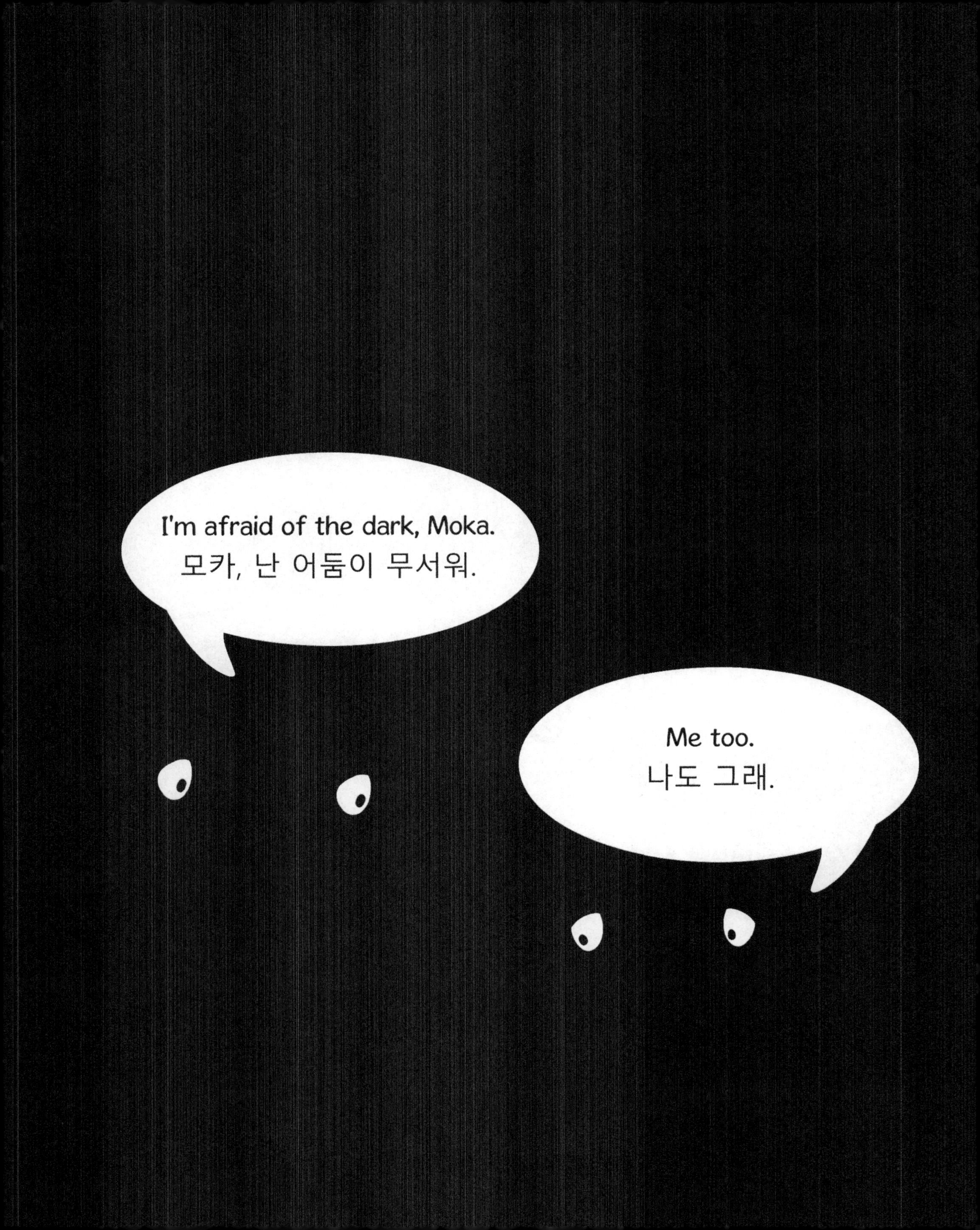
I'm afraid of the dark, Moka.
모카, 난 어둠이 무서워.
Me too.
나도 그래.

Tamara and Moka see their cat happily rubbing its paws against the teddy bear's fur.
타마라와 모카는 곰인형을 가지고 한참 신나게 노는 고양이를 발견합니다.

Can you hear anything, Tamara?
타마라, 무슨 소리 들려?
No, nothing at all.
아니, 아무것도.
Neither can I.
나도, 아무것도.

There are two flickering eyes in the corner. They're looking straight at us!
저기, 눈 두 개가 있어. 우리 쪽으로 달려드는 것 같아!
What do you think it is? A wizard?
저게 뭘까? 혹시... 마녀는 아닐까?
Turn the light on!
불 켜봐!

Aren't you going to close your eyes, Moka?
모카, 왜 눈을 안 감아?
Me too.
나도 그래.
No, I'm afraid of the dark.
난 어둠이 무서워.

There doesn't seem to be a ghost in the room. Tamara looks out the window and sees an owl perched on a branch. It's hooting happily with all its heart.

방 안에는 유령이 없습니다. 타마라는 창문 너머를 바라봅니다. 올빼미 한 마리가 나뭇가지 위에 앉아 정답게 울고 있습니다. 오올 오올-

It's only an owl, Moka! Anyway, ghosts don't exist.

모카, 저건 올빼미야! 유령은 없어.

Hey, look, there's another one!

아, 저기 좀 봐. 한 마리가 더 있어!

They must be in love! They're cuddling each other. You can turn the light off now.

둘이 사랑하는 사이인가 봐! 뽀뽀해주고 있잖아. 이제 불을 끄자.

CLICK 끅

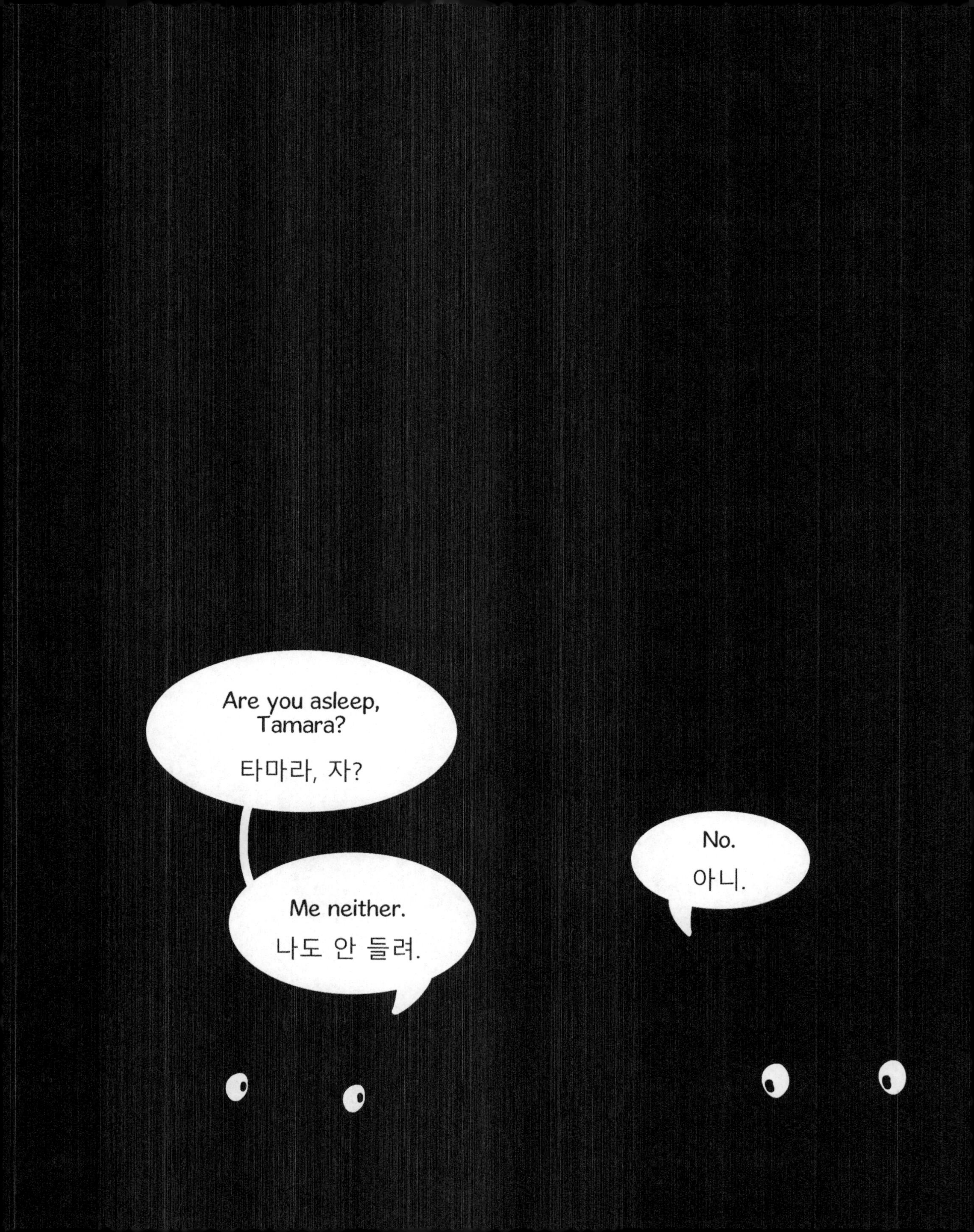
Are you asleep, Tamara?
타마라, 자?
No.
아니.
Me neither.
나도 안 들려.

Can you hear anything, Tamara?
타마라, 무슨 소리 안 들려?
No.
아니.
Me neither.
나도 안 들려.

Moka doesn't move. He pretends to be scared stiff. Tamara is scared too, but she bravely looks around a little so that she can see the monster behind her. And what does she see on her bedroom wall? The shadow of her head and it's ten times bigger than normal. Her Bantu knots are enormous and her ears seem to be sticking out more than ever.

"Very funny!"
"Hee, hee, hee!"

모카는 무서워서 온몸이 굳어버린 듯 옴짝달싹 못 합니다.
잔뜩 겁에 질린 채로, 그렇지만 간신히 용기를 내어 타마라는 살금살금 고개를 뒤로 돌려 괴물을 확인합니다. 뒤에는 뭐가 있을까요? 타마라의 머리보다 열 배는 더 커 보이는 그림자가 있네요. 촘촘히 땋은 머리와 동그란 두 귀가 그 어느 때보다 더 불쑥 튀어나와 보여요.

- 치, 장난 하는 거야?
- 히히히!

Tamara doesn't feel like talking anymore.
She's angry. She's angry with Moka for making
fun of her and she's angry because she walked
into her brother's trap.

타마라는 이제 말이 없습니다.
뾰로통해졌습니다. 자기를 놀린 모카에게,
그리고 모카의 장난을 진짜로 믿은 자신에게
화가 많이 납니다.

Moka doesn't feel like talking either. Or laughing.
But he's smiling, pleased with himself for having
played a trick on his sister.

모카도 말이 없고, 소리 내어 웃지도 않습니다.
침대 속에서 슬쩍 미소를 지어봅니다. 동생을
골탕먹인 게 즐거웠나 봐요.

The moon travels on through the night sky, distancing herself
from Tamara and Moka. The two children have too much
imagination for her liking. Monsters, ghosts and wizards.
Really! Everyone knows they don't exist.

두 아이의 상상이 지나쳐서일까요? 달님은 타마라와
모카의 방을 나와 멀리 저 하늘 속으로 여행을 떠납니다.
괴물과 유령과 마녀는 없어요. 어디에도 없어요!

We can't see the children's eyes in the dark anymore.
But we can hear something. What could it be? Have a guess.
You're right! Two little mouths snoring gently.

어둠 속에서 이제는 아이들의 눈이 보이지 않습니다.
그런데, 무슨 소리가 들리지 않나요?
아주 살며시 코고는 소리...

Author: Dominique Curtiss
Illustrator: Muriel Gestin
Translation into English: Rowland Hill
Translation into Korean: Hyonhee LEE

ISBN : 978-2-89687-747-8
Legal deposit: 2nd semester 2018
Bibliothèque et Archives nationales du Québec
Library and Archives Canada
Text©Dominique Curtiss 2018
Illustrations©Muriel Gestin 2018
Copyright©Chouetteditions.com 2018

Printed in Great Britain
by Amazon

57592130R00020